SHallow
in THE DEEP
EnD

www.ilf.org.au

Omnibus Books
an imprint of Scholastic Australia Pty Ltd (ABN 11 000 614 577)
PO Box 579, Gosford NSW 2250.
www.scholastic.com.au

Part of the Scholastic Group
Sydney • Auckland • New York • Toronto • London • Mexico City •
New Delhi • Hong Kong • Buenos Aires • Puerto Rico

First published in 2017.
Text copyright © Tiwi College Alalinguwi Jarrakarlinga, 2017.
Illustrations copyright © Tiwi College Alalinguwi Jarrakarlinga, 2017.

National Library of Australia Cataloguing-in-Publication entry

Title: Shallow in the deep end / written and illustrated by Tiwi
College Alalinguwi Jarrakarlinga with
Jared Thomas.
ISBN: 9781742762692 (paperback)
Target Audience: For primary school age.
Subjects: Pets--Juvenile fiction.
Dogs--Juvenile fiction.
Water buffalo--Juvenile fiction.
Tiwi Islands (N.T.)--Juvenile fiction
Other Creators/Contributors:
Tiwi College Alalinguwi Jarrakarlinga, author, illustrator.
Thomas, Jared, author, illustrator.

Typeset in Janson Text.
Printed in Australia by Griffin Press.
Scholastic Australia's policy, in association with Griffin Press,
is to use papers that are renewable and made
efficiently from wood grown in responsibly managed forests,
so as to minimise its environmental footprint.

10 9 8 7 6 5 4 3 2 1   17 18 19 20 21 / 1

SHALLOW in the DEEP END

Written and Illustrated by Tiwi College

Alalinguwi Jarrakarlinga

with Jared Thomas

An Omnibus Book from Scholastic Australia

One day I was watching a movie called *101 Dalmatians*, which is a movie about dogs. Lots of dogs.

I was very interested in the movie because I got to learn about the different species of dogs and how to care for them. I really enjoyed watching the movie and seeing how the dogs were cared for.

I thought that having a dog as a pet was a good idea because . . . well, I really wanted a dog as a pet.

Mum was making cupcakes in the kitchen and I ran over with excitement to ask if she could get me a dog.

I explained why I wanted a dog. I told Mum that dogs can be the friendliest, cuddliest and most loveable things.

Mum replied, 'No, you can't have a dog, you've got school work to do and I don't have time to look after it.'

I pleaded, 'Mum, please, please, please!'

But Mum kept saying 'NO, Erica!'

I turned round and slammed the cupboard door because I was angry with Mum for saying I couldn't have a dog.

Mum yelled at me and said, 'Go to your room now and don't get out until your dad returns from hunting pigs and magpie geese for us to eat.'

I walked in to my room and thought to myself that it would be better if I asked Dad to get me a dog.

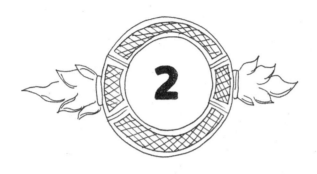

So the next day I rode my BMX bike along the beach, feeling the cool breeze blowing through my hair and then I rode through the bushland to find Dad, who was at work, working as the park ranger.

'*Awana*, bub. What are you doing here?'

'I just came to say hello,' I said, handing him some turtle stew that I got from my big cousin.

'Hmmm, my favourite,' he said, 'What's this for?'

'Just because I love you, Daddy,' I told him.

He raised his eyebrow and asked gruffly, 'What's really up? What have you done, Erica?'

'Nothing, Dad,' I said. I sat there with him while he ate his lunch for a while and then I asked, 'Dad, can I please have a puppy?'

Dad looked at me, smiled and said, 'I don't think so but I'll talk with your mum about it.'

'Thanks, Dad. *Nimpangi*,' I said.

Dad kissed me on the cheek and as soon as I was out of eyesight, I wiped it off.

3

Dad went out shooting to get us some
food, and he saw something running
through the bushes. He thought it was a
dingo but then a little buffalo appeared.
He followed the buffalo and found its
mother dead by the road. He wasn't sure if
it had been bitten by a dingo or a snake, or

hit by a four-wheel drive.

I was sitting on the veranda when
Dad pulled up in his land cruiser. 'Hey,
daughter, look what I've got for you,' he
said with a big smile on his face.

'What is it?' I asked before he opened
the car door.

'It's a dog,' he said.

'No it's not, it's a water buffalo.'

'It's a dog,' he told me again.

'If that's a dog, I'm treating her like a dog,' I told him.

'And I'm calling her Shallow.'

Dad nodded and said, 'Fair enough.'

'Welcome to Milikapiti, Shallow,' I said.

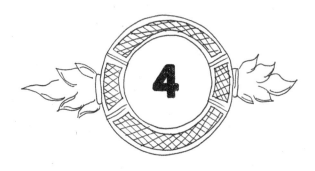

4

When me and my friend Izzy were going to school, she asked me if I would look after her dog Bruno while she went to Darwin for a couple of weeks to spend time with her family.

Bruno is a brown and yellow bull terrier that looks mean with his sharp teeth, but really he's a friendly dog that doesn't like humbug.

Izzy trusted me to look after Bruno because she knew how much I wanted a dog and thought it would be an opportunity to prove to my parents that I could look after a dog. And she knew I already had Shallow.

Even though I had Shallow, I was really nervous because I'd never looked after a real dog before. I had looked after my little sister Missy and when I did she messed up the kitchen. She turned on the stove and emptied all the cornflakes in the kitchen, the lounge room and her bedroom.

Izzy said that I had to feed Bruno every morning and night and play with him so that he can be healthy and grow stronger.

But Bruno knew that I would take good care of him because I'd known him since he was a puppy.

'*Kuwa*, I can do that.' I told Izzy.

'I trust you to look after my precious Bruno,' Izzy replied.

Izzy gave me some money to buy some dog food and also a mat for Bruno to sleep on.

Izzy gave me a hug and said

'*Nimpangi,* see ya in a few weeks time.'

'*Nimpangi,*' I said to Izzy.

Bruno followed me home and when

he saw Shallow eating grass on the

back lawn he quickly ran towards her. I

watched Bruno sniff around Shallow to

find out what she was like. Shallow was surprised and shocked when Bruno was sniffing around her, and they both stared at each other for a minute or two.

Then the animals began to play, and chase and follow each other around.

I couldn't believe my eyes.

5

That night, as Bruno was settling in, I treated Shallow just as if she were a dog too. I set up a food and water bowl in the laundry and I gave her coco pops.

The next day Bruno got into a fight with some other dogs. He does that sometimes.

Shallow saw Bruno in trouble so she ran over as fast as she could to help.

That night, I couldn't find Shallow in the yard. I was worried that she was missing. I went looking for her and found her cuddling up with Bruno in the laundry.

I've never seen dogs and water buffalos that close before.

From that day on, Bruno and Shallow became very close friends. Shallow was deeply in love with Bruno because Bruno didn't treat Shallow like the other dogs in Milikapiti.

I felt happy because Shallow had a friend to roam around with.

Shallow also started trying to fit in with all the kids and the dogs in the street.

But the other dogs seemed really angry with Shallow for trying to be like them when she was really a baby water buffalo.

I thought that if I kept treating Shallow like a dog, I would never have to replace her. And it would mean that Bruno would never get into fights because he had Shallow as his protection.

I was wrong.

The next day, Bruno and Shallow got into a fight against a pack of dogs.

Bruno and Shallow were winning the fight, but then more dogs came rushing for them and jumped on them. Then two ugly bony dogs bit Shallow's right leg.

Shallow's leg was badly injured. I decided to sneak out of the house that night when my parents were busy and take Shallow to the clinic, to get her some help.

The eyes of all the clinic staff popped out of their heads when they saw her.

'Can you treat my dog please?' I asked one of the nurses.

She was confused. 'That isn't a dog,' she said. 'That's a water buffalo!'

'But my dad said it's a dog!'

Shallow was at the clinic for two hours. She got an injection and stitched up.

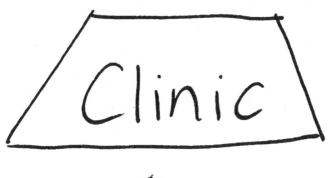

Shallow and I finally made our way back from the clinic, and when Bruno spotted us at the bus stop he started running towards us.

He had been at home worrying sadly about his beloved Shallow.

As Bruno was running, he saw Shallow limping, and the huge bandage wrapped around her right leg.

When Bruno finally reached us, he was so excited to see Shallow and me, that he gave me a soft bump and Shallow a big watery lick on her sore leg.

When we got back to the house Mum
and Dad were waiting on the couch with
an angry look on their faces.

'Where have you been for the last
three hours?' Mum asked.

I explained the whole reason why I wasn't at home including the fight, the clinic, how the nurses didn't understand that Shallow was a dog, and how Bruno was so worried.

Mum and Dad were still upset that Shallow and I went to the clinic without them knowing.

But they were happy that we were back home safely.

On Thursday afternoon I was sitting in
the car as Dad dropped oysters, mudcrab
and mud mussels to my Amawu down at
the big shady tree where lots of old ladies
with grey hair sat in a circle, playing
cards. It was off pay week and they were
desperate to win money.

Bruno started following Dad towards the card ring and I started whispering to him, 'Come back, Bruno,' because it was forbidden for anyone to interrupt the card game.

As the sun set, the dogs barked when they saw Bruno sitting behind Amawu.

Her friend Gracey was having good luck and winning biggest mobs of money.

The dogs started growling at Bruno and running towards him.

Suddenly I heard a stomping noise coming from behind a tree.

It was Shallow.

She ran towards Bruno to protect him.
Some of the old ladies had walking
frames. One of them looked up to see
Shallow charging and the old man from
the pink house yelled out, '*Awi*, that
buffalo is running there now!'

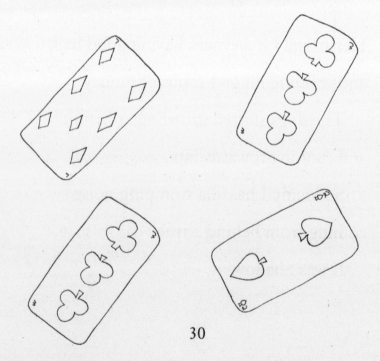

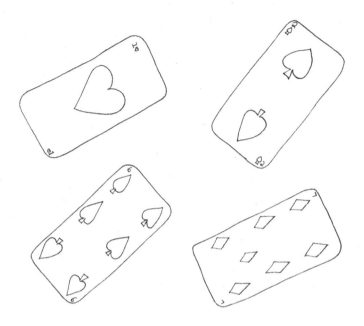

The old ladies jumped up in fright, throwing their money and cards in the air and grabbing their walking frames and sticks they hobbled for their lives.

Old Gracey waved her walking stick at Shallow and cursed her.

Embarrassed, I hid in the car so that no one could see me.

On a really hot afternoon, my little sister Missy kept begging me to pump up the pool that Mum and Dad got her for her birthday. I tried to ask my brother for help but he wouldn't listen so I went and got the pool from out of the storage area and I pumped it up myself.

As I was filling it up with water, I took Missy inside and we both got changed into our bathers.

Missy was so excited when she put on her floaties but when we walked outside of the house, she got hysterical.

Shallow and Bruno were in Missy's swimming pool.

Missy stood there screaming and Bruno must have thought she wanted to play because he started scratching on the plastic. Shallow began poking the side of the pool with her horns as if to say, 'Come on in, the water is beautiful.'

Suddenly the pool started to shrink. Shallow had popped the swimming pool with her horns. The pool looked like melted ice-cream on hot concrete.

When Mum found out she growled at me, saying, 'You need to save your pocket money and buy your little sister another swimming pool.'

I felt so angry because it wasn't my fault. It was Shallow and Bruno's fault.

It made me think that Dad needed to make Shallow her own little waterhole, then she could swim without popping anything.

9

Izzy came back from Darwin and then went to the boarding school at Tiwi College in Pickataramoor.

Bruno and Shallow couldn't be kept apart so Izzy asked if I could keep looking after Bruno – feeding him every morning and night and playing with him and Shallow so that they could be healthy and grow stronger.

I must have been doing a good job. Shallow had grown really big and was almost an adult.

Sometimes Shallow and Bruno would head down to see me at school.

During the morning break, Shallow and Bruno were in the bushes watching us kids do flips on the trampoline.

Most Tiwi kids are deadly at doing flips on the trampoline. We can do backflips, front flips, every trick there is to do.

Shallow and Bruno were getting the hang of it, watching us from the bushes.

They waited until the recess bell sounded and we went into class and then Shallow and Bruno each jumped on the trampoline.

Andy walked out of the classroom, around the admin building towards the bubblers.

He couldn't believe it when he saw Shallow and Bruno doing flips on the trampoline.

He raced back into his classroom and said, '*Awi*, you mob, come, come! LOOK, a buffalo and dog *la* trampoline bouncing away doing flips.'

All the boys yelled, 'You liar!'

I wondered if Shallow had popped the trampoline.

When the lunch bell rang Andy dragged everyone out to the trampolines to show them.

But Shallow and Bruno weren't there.

The trampolines were all broken with holes in them and everyone saw the buffalo and dog tracks around the base of the trampoline.

I walked away.

10

The footy grand final was in March and it was being played on the Tiwi Islands between the Muluwurri Magpies and The Tuyu Buffalos.

Dad was playing for the Magpies and thousands of people gathered to watch

the game. They had come on the ferry
and flew from Darwin and from all over
the country to watch the game.

Even Shallow had jumped on the back
of a tray back car and got a lift to the
grand final.

At half time both teams had a break

and the coaches were screaming at them.

It was a really tough and close game.
Tuyu were leading by two points.

During the last quarter, Dad was
lining up for a set shot at the goal
from the 50 metre mark and I was
cheering like crazy with all the Magpies
supporters.

The Tuyu supporters were booing.

Shallow jumped out of the car and saw
Bruno on the opposite side of the oval.
She began to run really fast across the
oval towards him.

Dad launched a torpedo punt through
the air. It soared towards the goal post.
But it frightened Shallow. She jumped up
and attacked the ball with her horns and

popped it.

Everyone got really upset and started chasing Shallow, so she ran off to Bruno to get his help. But even Bruno was disappointed at her for ruining the game.

At last the umpire found another ball and the game started again.

The Magpies won the grand final but Dad and Mum were still fed up with Shallow and Bruno.

11

Since Shallow had arrived, she had got into fights, needed to be taken to the clinic, broke Missy's swimming pool, made all of the nannas angry when she crashed through their card game, ruined the trampoline and wrecked the football grand final.

I really did try to do my best looking
after Shallow but she wouldn't listen. She
was a run-amok water buffalo.

One day, Dad came home from work
and said, 'Erica, I have to take Shallow

back to her mob.'

I was really sad but I understood that
Shallow was getting all grown up and
would be happier back in the bush, with

her mob.

Bruno looked so sad. He sat on the blanket where he and Shallow used to cuddle up when they were little fellas. I tried to bring him good tucker to cheer him up but nothing seemed to work.

But then Izzy came home from boarding school and said, 'Thanks for looking after Bruno, I hope he was a good fella,' and Bruno came bouncing out of the house and almost knocked Izzy off her feet, he was so happy to see her.

I sat around bored on my veranda

watching the world go by but nothing much seemed to happen without Shallow and Bruno.

And then, one night, Dad pulled up in his land cruiser and said, 'Hey daughter, look what I've got you.'

I looked up and couldn't believe it, a beautiful little Chihuahua. I named her Lucy.

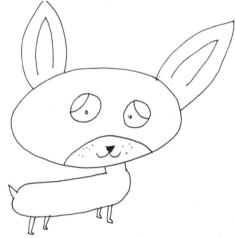

I still miss Shallow and Bruno but at least I still get to see Bruno when I visit Izzy. And every time I see a water buffalo it reminds me of Shallow and all the crazy times we had.

Tiwi Islands

The Tiwi Islands are made up of two islands that are located about 80 kilometres north of Darwin. These are Bathurst and Melville islands. The population of Tiwi is about 2,500 people. On the Melville side there are communities Pirlangimpi and Milikapiti. There are also two communities on Bathurst Island, Ranku and Wurrimiyanga. To get to the Tiwi Islands you can either catch a small plane which takes twenty to thirty minutes or take a ride on the ferry which takes about two hours. There are many places for fishing and hunting and we have lovely beaches, but you can't go for a swim because we have too many big crocodiles.

TIWI COLLEGE

Our school Tiwi College is located at Pickataramoor,
which is on Melville Island. Tiwi College is a
boarding facility where students are accommodated
in Family Group Homes from Monday to Friday.
Our school isn't big: we only have five classrooms and
about seventy students. The students from Melville
Island catch a bus or a troopy from their community
to school which takes one to two hours. The kids
that live on Bathurst Island have to catch a boat to
get to Melville Island then jump in a troopy to get to
school, which takes about an hour. During the wet
season the roads get really boggy and turn into rivers.
This can mean it takes a long time to get to school.

INDIGENOUS LITERACY FOUNDATION

The Indigenous Literacy Foundation aims to make a positive difference to the lives of Australian Aboriginal and Torres Strait Islander children by focusing on ways to improve their literacy. We believe that a young child's future educational experiences can be greatly improved through enjoyable and positive engagements with books in the family and community environment at an early age. This book was produced as part of the Indigenous Literacy Foundation's Create Initiative. The initiative partners young Indigenous women with publishers and mentors to create (produce stories), cultivate (build knowledge) and motivate (grow self-esteem).

 Find out more about ILF's work at www.ilf.org.au

JARED THOMAS

Jared is a writer of theatre and children's and young adult fiction. His novel *'Sweet Guy'* was shortlisted for the South Australian and Victorian Premier's Literary Awards and his children's novel *'Dallas Davis, the Scientist and the City Kids'* was published in the Oxford University Press 'Yarning Strong' series. *'Calypso Summer'* won the 2013 State Library of Queensland Black&Write Fellowship, was shortlisted in the 2014 Victorian Premier's Literary Award for Indigenous Writing and was included in the 2015 International Youth Library White Ravens list – given to books that deserve worldwide attention because of their universal themes and exceptional artistic and literary style and design. *'Songs that Sound like Blood,'* is Jared's latest, and the 'Game Day' basketball series co-written with Patty Mills will be released in 2017.

His professional career has included roles such as Manager, Aboriginal and Torres Strait

Islander Arts for Arts South Australia, and lecturer at the University of South Australia.

In 2016 Jared mentored Tiwi College students through the Indigenous Literacy Foundation's *Create Initiative*.